MASTERS OF THE SWOONIVERSE

T SHREWMAN

PUFFIN

CONTENTS

Chapter 1

THE GHOSTLY GOOEY GALLEON

First Officer Ooze checked the *Rhapsody 2*'s ZPS readings.

'Great gloops! I've found something, Captain,' he called.

'You've located Chief Engineer Splutnik, the last of our missing crew members?' the captain asked hopefully as he crossed the spaceship's bridge to join Ooze at the controls.

'Not yet, Captain,' said Ooze. 'But the ZPS has located a replacement steering device for the one that was damaged when we crash-landed here on Music Island.'

'Well, that's a start,' replied the captain. 'But it's useless if we can't find Splutnik! We need the entire crew aboard to power the ship and continue our mission to investigate that mysterious growing star.'

'That star continues to have a disastrous effect on the Moshi world,' added Dr. C. Fingz, the *Rhapsody 2*'s chief medical officer. 'The closer it gets, the faster the snow on Mount Sillimanjaro melts and the higher the water levels rise. We must investigate before Monstro City finds itself underwater! Where's this steering device located, Ooze?'

Ooze checked his coordinates.

'It's in the ocean, east of Music Island,' he said. 'Onboard some kind of ancient floaty thing made of wood.'

'I'll summon the Super Moshis,' said Squirk.

'It's a ship,' said Zommer as the Super Moshis' dinghy neared its destination.

'No, it's a pirate ship! Look, the name's written on the side,' exclaimed Diavlo.

'The *Gooey Galleon*,' said Luvli, reading the writing.

'Oh, terrific. Pirates,' moaned Furi.

They pulled in alongside the pirate ship.

'Ahoy, matey dudes!' Zommer called up. 'Throw us down ye rope ladder. We want to come aboard!'

'Ahoy? Ye?' Poppet giggled. 'What are you talking about, Zom?'

'I'm speaking Olde Piratey,' said Zommer. 'They won't understand us otherwise.'

'Yeah, well, I'm not sure that real pirates talk that way. It's only in storyboo–'

A face suddenly appeared over the side of the *Gooey Galleon.*

'Aaaaaarrrrr! Ahoy to ye all!' it hollered, flinging down a rope ladder. 'Come aboard, me hearties.'

Poppet's eyes widened.

'Wow. Guess I was wrong,' she laughed.

The Super Moshis stood in silence on the deck of the ship and tried not to gawk at the pirate standing before them. It was strange. In almost every respect he looked exactly as a pirate should look. Except he was completely see-through!

'Arrrr see ye never met a ghost pirate a'fore,' he chuckled. 'Jaunty Jack be me name. Arrrr'm first mate of the *Gooey Galleon*. What can we be doin' for ye, me hearties?'

'We're the Super Moshis and we've come to ask you a big favour,' said Poppet, smiling sweetly.

'What be this favourrrrrr?' Jaunty Jack asked.

Poppet nodded towards the large wooden steering wheel in the middle of the deck.

'Our friends' ship crashed and its steering wheel broke. We were wondering if we could possibly have yours . . . ?' she asked hopefully.

'Aaaarrrr sympathize with ye friends' situation,' Jaunty Jack said, his eyes misting over. 'We be havin' some problems of aaaarrrr own. Ever since we nabbed aaaarrrselves some booty from Hong Bong Island we be in the grip of a beastly curse.'

'What happened?' Poppet asked.

'We were the most feared pirates of the Seventy Seas until that fateful journey to Hong Bong,' said Jaunty Jack gravely. 'We had it all! We dined off golden platters. We ate with silver spoons. We slept on mattresses stuffed with Rox . . .'

'That sounds uncomfortable, dude,' Zommer whispered to Diavlo.

'. . . but it all changed after that accursed kitty came aboard,' Jaunty Jack continued. 'Since then the *Gooey Galleon* be marooned on this sandbank and we be goin' nowhere . . . '

'Great! So you won't need that steering wheel, then,' said Furi happily.

The Super Moshis all frowned at Furi.

'Whaaaaaat? What did I say?' Furi asked, confused.

Katsuma rolled his eyes and turned back to Jack.

'You have a cat problem?' he asked.

'Tingaling, the Kitten of Good Fortune, they call her,' Jack said with a sigh. 'She be part of the Hong Bong Island booty, but she ain't brought us nothin' but misery.'

He hung his ghostly head mournfully.

'That's a real shame, Jack,' said Furi, shaking his head. 'But you really won't be needing that steering wheel, then, will you?'

Jaunty Jack looked up and his face suddenly broke into a smile.

'Har har! Ye be right, matey. Ye can have it and good luck to ye!'

While Katsuma and Poppet busied themselves undoing the bolts that held the ship's steering wheel in place, the rest of the Supers chatted to Jaunty Jack.

'It's very quiet onboard the *Gooey Galleon*,' said Diavlo. 'Where's the rest of the crew?'

'We be havin' a big belchin' contest this aaaaarrrrfternoon, so Captain Codswallop and the rest of the crew be preparin',' explained Jack.

'Ahoy!' someone cried from the crow's nest high above the deck. The Supers looked up in surprise.

'Speakin' of one of the rascally devils . . . ' chuckled Jack. 'Here be McScruff. Hold on to ye masks, Super Moshis, he's been acting mighty strange since that cat came aboard!'

McScruff suddenly grabbed a rope and slid down it towards Katsuma and Poppet.

'WHEEEEEEEEEE!' he cried, his red spotted bandana fluttering in his wake.

'What in marine madness is this?' Katsuma yelled as McScruff bared his teeth and grabbed the steering wheel from his paws.

'Come back with that!' Poppet cried, trying to swipe it back.

But McScruff was too quick. He shot up out of reach and flung the steering wheel into the sea!

Everyone rushed to the side of the ship and watched

in horror as it disappeared beneath the waves.

'Aaaaarrrrr,' said Jaunty Jack, frowning. 'That'll go right to the bottom of the Potion Ocean and it's verrrrrry deep. Looks like you'll be needin' our divin' suit, me Supers . . . if ye can find it.'

'What do you mean if?' asked Luvli, but Jack didn't have a chance to answer.

'By the powers of King Neptune and aaarrrrll his fishy friends, where aaarrrrr you, Jack?' screamed a voice from the captain's cabin.

Jaunty Jack immediately snapped to attention.

'That's Captain Codswallop! Aaarrr better go!' he said, floating off speedily and disappearing through the wall.

Poppet sighed. 'So that means we've got to find this diving suit, fetch the steering wheel from the bottom of the sea and . . . Furi, would you please stop making that silly noise and pay attention?'

'It's not me, Poppet,' said Furi. 'I thought it was Diavlo.'

'Me?' Diavlo huffed. 'Don't be a furry fool!'

Luvli cleared her throat. 'It's not any of us,' she said. 'The noise is coming from over there.' Luvli pointed at the carved green figurehead at the prow of the ship. Its head was trapped in a diving helmet and it was squealing for help.

Chapter 2

PAYING PIRATE DUES

'Looks like we've found the first part of the diving suit,' said Katsuma. 'But that helmet is really wedged on. How do we get it off?'

The Super Moshis gathered around the figurehead and were pondering what to do when Poppet spotted something useful hanging from the mast.

'Look, it's a Moshling – Blurp the Batty Bubblefish. How cute!'

'Dude, he's all, like, puffed up with nowhere to blow!' said Zommer, looking at the puffy fish with amusement.

Luvli flew over to unhook the little Moshling from the beam. 'I think I know how we could use those little lungs,' she said. She fluttered over to the metal helmet and attached the Blurp to the end of the air pipe coming out of it. With a little nudge from Poppet,

the Moshling blew all the air out of its puffy cheeks, through the pipe and up into the helmet – and the pressure blew it clean off the figurehead with a 'pop'! Furi picked it up and tucked it under his arm.

'Hoist the sails, I'm free at last, thank you!' the figurehead exclaimed as she blinked her long eyelashes at the Supers. 'My name's Mavis, by the way.'

Poppet smiled and introduced herself and the other Super Moshis.

'Were you trying to tell us something before?' she added. 'Through the helmet?'

'Was I?' Mavis thought for a moment. 'Oh yes, I remember now! I saw what that naughty McScruff did and I wanted to tell you that the boots for the diving suit are in Captain Codswallop's cabin.'

'Ahhh, thanks for the info, dude.' Zommer grinned. 'One thing though bro, why were you wearing that diving helmet? It looked waaaaay uncomfortable!'

'Those pesky poltergeists put it on me,' she sighed. 'They've been cursed ever since Tingaling the Kitten of Good Fortune was brought onboard.'

'So we saw. We'll do what we can to save the *Gooey Galleon*, we promise,' said Katsuma gravely. 'But first we have to get that steering wheel.'

The Super Moshis nodded in agreement and made their way over to the captain's cabin.

'Come in ye landlubbers and make yerselves useful!' the captain cried as the Super Moshis piled through the door.

'Useful?' Furi looked around in confusion.

'No guest can leave until they pay their dues. I've a belching contest about to start and I needs ye to find me food. I gots no wind in me sails, if ye know what

arrr mean!' the captain said, pacing around his cabin. Jaunty Jack hovered nearby trying to keep out of his way.

'Food?' Katsuma asked hesitantly.

'The Captain here needs us to find him some food to make him gassy,' said Furi knowledgeably. 'That way he'll be sure to beat the rest of the crew in the Battle of the Burps.'

'Ewwww, gross!' Poppet wrinkled her nose.

'Ye got to pay ye dues on my boat, landlubbers!' the captain thundered. 'Find me fuel and I'll think about lending ye me boots . . . '

Katsuma looked startled and the captain leered at him.

'Aye, ye didn't think arrr knew what ye were wanting eh?' he chuckled. 'Aaaarrrr've got me spies.'

The captain looked meaningfully at Jaunty Jack.

Katsuma frowned.

'Fine, we'll help you,' he replied. 'Then we get the diving boots.'

'Deal!' the captain laughed, shaking Katsuma by the paw.

Jaunty Jack coughed in an embarrassed way. 'Captain Codswallop stashed his midnight snacks aaaarrrrll around his cabin and now he can't remember where he put 'em,' he explained. 'Ye'll need to search high an' low to find 'em.'

'Let's do this, Super Moshis!' Poppet said encouragingly.

While the adventurers searched for the captain's snacks, Katsuma made an interesting discovery. Hanging from a hook in the ceiling was a locked cage and inside that cage was Tingagling, the Kitten of Good Fortune!

'She be all locked up tight in there!' Jaunty Jack whispered

to Katsuma. 'Unfortunately, the key to the padlock mysteriously disappeared . . . '

'Interesting . . . ' Katsuma said quietly.

Poppet appeared by his side.

'Here's your Gloop Soup, Chicken Drummer, Hooti Fruiti Juice and Ice-Scream, Captain Codswallop,' she said, handing him the food. Zommer had to hold Furi back as he eyed the delicious snacks hungrily.

'Aaaarrrr, I thank ye, me Moshi mateys, for all ye help!' the captain said as he hurriedly scoffed down the food. 'The quicker ye eat, the better the belching benefits!'

The Supers all took a step backwards in case the captain chose to demonstrate his burping expertise.

'Epic, so we can have the diving boots now?' Zommer asked.

'Ye dues are paid, so help yeselves,' replied the captain, rubbing his belly as he slowly faded into thin air. 'I gots a contest to win!'

Poppet grabbed the boots.

'We've got the boots and the helmet. Now we just

need to find the suit,' she said. 'But this is a big ship and we don't know where to look!'

'Aaarrr think aaarrr can help you there,' said Jaunty Jack with a grin. 'Hoisted up the mainsail be the suit. Climb the ladder to the crow's nest and ye shall find it, Supers!'

'Phoof! That was a looooong climb!' Furi puffed as he squished into the tiny crow's nest along with the other Supers.

Katsuma looked up and saw the diving suit flapping in the breeze like a flag.

'And there's the suit, right where Jaunty Jack said it'd be,' he said, reaching over to grab the rope it hung from.

McScruff suddenly materialized beside him.

'What y'aaarrrrr doin', me Moshi matey?' he cackled.

'You're not getting this one, McScruff!' Katsuma cried, grabbing the rope and yanking the diving suit into the crow's nest.

McScruff's face fell.

'Arrrrr was only playin' with yer before!' he said disappointedly. 'Aaarrrrrm sorry about the steerin' wheel. Let me make it up to ye over a few bottles of cold Wobble-Ade!'

Zommer and Furi's faces lit up with interest, but Poppet frowned.

'Hmmm, thanks, McScruff, but we're in a bit of a hurry,' she said as Diavlo and Luvli untied the diving suit and stashed it in Poppet's backpack.

'OK, let's go,' said Luvli, flying out of the crow's nest with Diavlo. Katsuma and Poppet hurried down the ladder back to the deck. Zommer and Furi, however, stayed put.

'I don't know why we had to climb up here,' grumbled Furi. 'It's a long way up . . . and down! Thirsty work, all that climbing . . . '

'Yeah! I'd say we, like, totally deserve a Wobble-Ade . . .' Zommer said.

McScruff grinned and opened a small chest in the corner of the crow's nest. Inside were several bottles of icy-cold Wobble-Ade.

'Help yerselves, me parched pals,' he winked.

Furi and Zommer didn't need any more encouragement. Just as quickly as you can say, 'swig and swallow', they'd both downed an entire bottle of Wobble-Ade each!

'BUUUUURRRRRRP! Most excellent!' Zommer laughed as he wiped his mouth.

'I think I can tackle that BUUUURRRP – I mean *rope* ladder now,' snickered Furi.

'Ye're a couple of mighty fine belchers!' cried McScruff. 'Take arrrr couple for ye climb and make sure to watch the belching contest later!' McScruff insisted, handing them a bottle of Wobble-Ade each.

Furi and Zommer gratefully popped the bottles into their backpacks and hoisted themselves out of the crow's nest and onto the rope ladder.

'Hey, McScruff was a gnarly dude in the end, huh?' Zommer called to Furi.

'I agree! He's completely misunderstood!' Furi hollered back.

Chapter 3

THE KITTEN OF GOOD FORTUNE

Meanwhile on deck, Katsuma realized they had a problem. With all the ghost pirates busy with the belching contest, they didn't have anyone who knew how to work the safety winch.

'You need the winch to drop the diver overboard and get them out again,' Mavis explained. 'I can't do it. I haven't got any arms!'

'Who else is there to help if we can't ask the crew?' Luvli asked.

'Well . . . there is Tingaling the Kitten of Good

Fortune,' Mavis suggested. 'But she's locked up in that cage and the key is missing.'

'This is ridiculous! Someone must know where the key is!' Diavlo huffed. Then he spied the crewmembers of the *Gooey Galleon* on the opposite end of the deck and flew over to them, his fiery head burning hotter than usual.

'Uh-oh, Diavlo's getting angry . . . ' Poppet whispered as they watched their friend gesturing wildly at a ghost with hooks for hands.

'This looks bad,' muttered Katsuma as Diavlo flew back to join his friends, his face grim.

'Gah! Those stupid ghost pirates!' Diavlo snorted. 'They haven't lost the key to Tingaling's cage at all. The one with the hooks – Handy Van Hookz he calls himself – has swallowed it! He absolutely refuses to give it to us. They don't want to free Tingaling because they think it'll bring even worse luck!'

Just then, Furi and Zommer dropped back onto the deck.

'Ahoy-hoy!' Zommer laughed. 'What have we missed? Have we got the steering wheel yet?'

'Not yet,' said Katsuma. 'We've got a problem.'

'Well, let's have a little drink while we think – BARP! – ooh, excuse me!' Furi blushed as he burped loudly.

'A drink? Did you have some Wobble-Ade up there?' Luvli asked suspiciously.

'Yes,' grinned Furi. 'But don't worry, we've got another couple of bottles to share!'

'Excellent!' Katsuma smiled. 'Hand them over . . . I think I have a plan.'

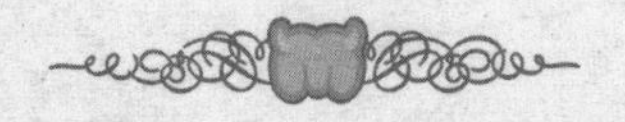

With two bottles of Wobble-Ade in hand, Katsuma made his way over to the pirate ghosts.

'Who's winning?' he asked.

'Aaaarrrr, it's anybody's game!' Captain Codswallop replied gleefully.

'Burrrrrrp!' Jaunty Jack belched.

'Arrrrr need more bubbles!' Handy Van Hookz said, rubbing his ghostly belly. The key to Tingaling's cage bobbed up and down inside him.

'Perhaps I can help . . . ?' Katsuma smiled, dangling the two bottles of Wobble-Ade in front of the ghost's face.

Handy's eyes widened in excitement.

'Arrrr don't mind if arrrr do!' he grinned, grabbing a bottle and guzzling the fizzy drink. The key sloshed around in his tummy as he did.

'Delicious doubloons!' he exclaimed, gulping the second bottle too.

Slowly but surely, the bubbles from the Wobble-Ade caused the key in Handy's tummy to shudder and shake.

'Now behold the power of the belch!' yelled Handy,

waving a hook to indicate that the Supers should stand back. The ghost opened his mouth wide and with a loud '**BAAAAAARRRRRPPPPP!!!**' the key came flying out of his mouth and hit the deck.

'Yar, I be the champion belcher,' cried Handy gleefully.

Captain Codswallop grinned. 'Crabsticks, that be a

powerful one indeed! I declare ye the winner!'

Katsuma picked up the key and wiped off the ghostly slobber.

'Thanks, Handy!' he said. But the ghost pirates weren't listening; they were too busy congratulating the excited Van Hookz on his record-breaking belch!

The Supers raced to the cabin and freed Tingaling, who squeaked a grateful meow and agreed to help the Supers with the winch on deck. There was only one thing left to do – decide who'd be lowered into the water to get the steering wheel.

'I think as a reward for providing the Wobble-Ade, Zommer or Furi should go down and get it,' said Poppet.

'Wait . . . that's a reward?' said Zommer.

'It's a very heroic thing to do,' Luvli added as she bundled him into the suit.

Zommer was just about to protest further when Diavlo shoved the helmet on his head and Katsuma squeezed his feet into the boots.

'OK, I'll do it!' Zommer's voice sounded muffled inside the helmet.

'Great! Thanks for volunteering, Zom,' said Furi.

Tingaling meowed as she took her place by the winch.

'Off you go!' Katsuma called as the Supers dangled Zommer over the side of the ship.

Slowly Tingaling unwound the rope and Zommer was lowered into the cold, black sea.

It was dark and spooky in the water and the deeper he went, the darker and spookier it got!

'Be cool,' he muttered to himself. 'Zommers aren't cowards. We're brave! We're strong! We're . . . OK . . . we are a little freaked out right now!'

Happily Zommers were also well known for being very easily distracted.

'Oooh, what's that? Radical!' he exclaimed.

Zommer could make out a glowing green light down on the sea floor. As he neared, it began to take shape.

'Is t-that a . . . TV?' he shouted in amazement. 'On the seabed?!'

'Shuuuuuuush!' someone hissed from below. 'You'll annoy you-know-who!'

Zommer wiped the smudged visor of the diving

helmet to try and see who was speaking to him. Sprawled on an overstuffed armchair with his eyes glued to the TV was a chubby green octopus. He was tapping away at a videogame control with his front two tentacles.

'Er . . . well . . . hey, man!' Zommer called brightly. 'I'm Zommer!'

The octopus sighed loudly.

'What did I just say?' he snapped, barely looking up

from his game. 'Ye're going to disturb the Beast if you don't shut up. And it gets very angry.'

'The Beast?' Zommer whispered as he plopped down on the sea floor.

The octopus gestured behind Zommer, who turned to peer into the darkness. Twenty metres away a small lantern swayed gently in the current. Its dim light illuminated something terrifying. A BIG UGLY MONSTER-FISH!

'Heavy hairballs! What is that?' Zommer squawked as

he took in the fish's massive fangs and googly green eyes.

The octopus grinned.

'That is the Beast,' he replied. 'It's already in a foul mood. Someone dropped that steering wheel right on its hooter and woke it up. Now it's lodged right in its 'orrible nostril.'

'Oh, r-r-really?' Zommer gulped nervously as the Beast peered at him in annoyance. 'And . . . like . . . what would it do if I . . . like . . . *did* disturb it?'

The octopus waved its tentacles in the air. Three of its tentacles were smaller than the others and had wooden stumps attached.

Zommer gasped in horror.

'Dude. It ate your tentacles? Gnarly . . .' he whispered fearfully.

'Huh? What? Oh, now look what you've made me do! I've lost a life in Super Mustachio Brothers!' The octopus threw down the joystick in disgust and stared angrily at Zommer. 'What were you saying?'

'Your tentacles . . . you got those wooden peg legs, bro . . . ' Zommer began hesitantly.

The octopus chuckled.

'Oh, I see! Nooooo, the Beast didn't chomp my tentacles. I've a nervous habit of chewing 'em myself! Hence the name – Octopeg! Pleased to meet you.'

Chapter 4

ZOMMER'S HEROIC MOMENT

'So, y'know that steering wheel that hit the Beast...' Zommer began hesitantly. 'There's been a killer mix-up onboard the *Gooey Galleon* and I totally need to get it back.'

'Good luck with that!' Octopeg said distractedly, returning to his game. 'Did you see where it landed? It's stuck on the Beast's nose. The only way you'll get that steering wheel back is if the Beast goes back to sleep. And the only way that's going to happen is if you can get the Classico Clams to sing their famous lullaby.'

Zommer swallowed.

‘Whoooooaaa. And where do I find the Classico Clams?’ he asked.

‘Over there,’ Octopeg nodded at a bunch of coral and clamshells on a nearby rock. ‘But they need a musical accompaniment and that’s the problem. The music box has broken into pieces and I’m not exactly good with my hands.’

Octopeg waved his non-game playing tentacles.

Zommer looked at his own two hands.

'I think I could totally fix it,' he said as he wiggled his nine fingers thoughtfully.

'You can try,' Octopeg said. 'The pieces are all over there somewhere.'

Zommer trotted over to where Octopeg had indicated, and with a little digging around found all the bits of the broken music box.

'Found them!' he called triumphantly, then sat down to piece it together.

'Back to Super Mustachio Brothers,' Octopeg replied, barely listening.

'He's been down there a long time,' said Furi anxiously.

The Super Moshis leaned over the railing of the *Gooey Galleon* and stared into the sea.

'If Tingaling isn't worried –' said Poppet, glancing over at the Kitten of Good Fortune dozing in a fluffy ball by the winch, ' – and she obviously isn't – then I'm not worried.'

'Ye-es, I suppose you're right . . .' Furi replied doubtfully.

'Done!' Zommer cried happily, as he put the finishing touches to the music box.

Octopeg frowned.

'Remember what I said about yelling?' he grumbled.

'Oh yeah, sorry, dude,' Zommer whispered in reply as he glanced at the Beast. Its eyes were half-closed, but Zommer got the impression it was watching him closely. 'What do I do now?' he asked.

'Wake up the Classico Clams and they'll do the rest,' said Octopeg.

Zommer bobbed over to the rock where the Classico Clams were stuck fast and placed the music box carefully in the middle of them. He slowly creaked open the lid and immediately beautiful music spilled out into the sea.

One by one, the Classico Clams opened their shells and began to sing, their voices harmonizing with the music to create a wonderful lullaby.

Zommer looked over at the Beast. Its eyes looked heavy and its lids slowly began to close.

'I think it's working,' said Zommer in a hushed voice.

'Of course it's working.' Octopeg rolled his eyes. 'Just give it a minute to make sure the Beast is properly asleep and then you can –'

But Zommer didn't hear Octopeg's warning. He'd already snuck over to the dozing Beast and yanked the ship's steering wheel off its nose!

The Beast's eyes snapped open and it gnashed its ginormous fangs.

'Uh-oh . . .' Octopeg gasped. 'Now you've really done it!'

Zommer stared into the gaping mouth of the Beast and screeched in horror.

'Get out of here!' Octopeg yelled.

Quick as he could Zommer yanked on the winch rope, giving the agreed sign that Tingaling could start reeling him in. Almost immediately he was jerked upwards, out of reach of the Beast's jaws.

'Come on, Tingaling!' Zommer shrieked as the Beast swam out of its grotto and up towards him.

SNAP! Went its jaws, but once again Zommer was hauled up just beyond its reach, the steering wheel safely tucked under his arm.

'See ya, Octopeg!' Zommer called, as he hastily pulled his legs up out of the Beast's bite range. 'And thank yoooooou!'

SNAP! SNAP!

Octopeg watched, with a mixture of terror and amusement, as Zommer was pulled to the surface, the Beast only one bite behind him the whole way.

'And people ask me why I prefer video games!' he sighed, resuming his game.

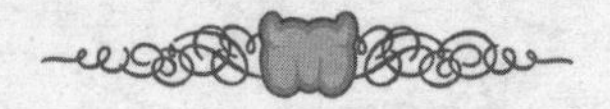

The Super Moshis cheered with relief as Zommer broke the surface.

'Get me out of here!' he cried, thrashing about on the rope. 'There's a fish on my tail!'

Tingaling wound the winch as fast as her little paws could go and Zommer was soon halfway up the side of the *Gooey Galleon*.

'Since when was Zom frightened of –' began Katsuma.

But the words stuck in his throat as the Beast reared out of the sea and snapped at the dangling Super Moshi.

The Supers jumped into action. Furi and Katsuma joining Tingaling on the winch, while Diavlo and Luvli flew over to haul Zommer, and the steering wheel, onto the ship.

'That thing wanted to gobble you up!' Poppet exclaimed as she watched the Beast disappear back into the sea.

'Don't I know it, dudette!' Zommer gasped as he yanked off the diving helmet and collapsed on the deck with relief.

The Super Moshis and Tingaling gathered around him, all offering their congratulations for being such a super superhero!

'I couldn't have done it without you, Tingaling.' Zommer grinned as he bent down to scratch the little Moshling's head.

'Arrrrr! And thanks to ye Super Moshis, we finally be free of the curse that has stricken our ship!' Captain Codswallop cried, as the entire crew of the *Gooey Galleon* appeared on deck.

'How do you know the curse has been lifted?' Diavlo asked.

'Arrr be feeling it in me ghostly guts,' Codswallop replied with a wink. Suddenly he let out a loud, wet

belch. **BARRRRRRRRRRP!** 'Or maybe it just be wind!' he added with a giggle.

Everyone burst into fits of laughter, including Tingaling, who was quite a sensible cat and didn't usually laugh at that sort of thing.

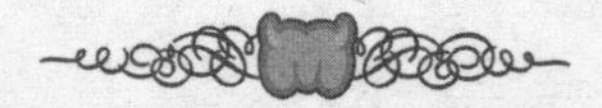

With the steering wheel and Tingaling safely stowed aboard their dinghy, the Super Moshis said goodbye to the ghostly pirate crew and rowed to shore.

Once they hit dry land, they quickly made their way on foot through the Unknown Zone and back to the Zoshling spaceship.

'I'm getting really worried about that star,' said Poppet quietly as she stared up at the ball of light in the sky. 'It's so close to our world now we don't even need a telescope to see it.'

'Don't worry, Poppet. Now that we've found the replacement steering wheel for the *Rhapsody 2*, the only thing left to do is find the ship's final missing crewmember,' Katsuma reassured her. 'Then the Zoshlings can continue their mission to unravel that galactic mystery.'

'I know you're right, Katsuma, but we're running out of time,' Poppet replied unhappily.

Chapter 5

WELCOME TO JOLLYWOOD

'Super Moshis!' Captain Squirk cried happily as the monsters entered the jungle clearing. He raced down the *Rhapsody 2*'s gangplank with Sprockett, Hubbs and the rest of the Zoshlings following behind him. 'We're so pleased to see you all!'

'Well, not pleased exactly,' grumbled Hubbs.

'But you told me you missed them,' said Sprockett in surprise.

'Shut up, you cretinous cog!' Hubbs snapped.

'It's great to see you all too,' smiled Luvli, ignoring Hubbs's grumpy outburst.

'We've got the steering wheel,' added Furi. 'Thanks to Zom.'

Zommer smiled shyly.

'It was team work,' he said, handing it over to First Officer Ooze.

'Wonderful!' the Zoshling exclaimed, examining the wooden steering wheel. 'It's an antique, but it'll do nicely.'

'We have some exciting news for you too, Super Moshis,' Squirk grinned. 'Dr. C. Fingz has been receiving garbled messages from a place called Jollywood. We think Chief Engineer Splutnik, our final crewmember, is there.'

'Jollywood? That's on the far western shores of Music Island,' Katsuma said. 'To save some time do you think you can, y'know, 'beam' us over there?'

Captain Squirk chuckled.

'Yes, of course! And as we've only got a few minor repairs to the *Rhapsody 2* to complete, I can spare Dr. C. Fingz to go with you. His psychic skills will come in handy in trying to track down Splutnik.'

'Sounds like an excellent plan!' Diavlo said. 'But

before we go, we have one final surprise for you all . . .'

Poppet carefully placed her backpack on the ground.

'What've you got in there?' Hubbs asked.

'Please say it's sandwiches!' Squirk squealed hopefully.

'Not quite . . .' said Diavlo, loosening the straps of the backpack. Two furry white paws emerged, followed by a fluffy little face.

'Is it edible?' Squirk asked uncertainly.

'It's a Moshling!' Hubbs exclaimed, reaching out his metallic arms to Tingaling. 'Come to Hubbsy, little kitty.'

Tingaling twitched her whiskers and wriggled her ears as if making up her mind. Then she jumped out of the backpack, raced over to Hubbs and rubbed happily against his wheel.

'It likes you, Hubbs,' said Sprockett.

'Course it does!' Hubbs said as he rubbed Tingaling's fluffy coat. 'Does kitty want some din-dins? You come with Hubbs and we'll find you something to eat.'

With that, Sprockett, Hubbs and Tingaling boarded the *Rhapsody 2*.

'Well!' Poppet said. 'I did not see that coming.'

The Zoshlings and the Supers all laughed in agreement. Sprockett and Hubbs were turning out to be nice guys after all!

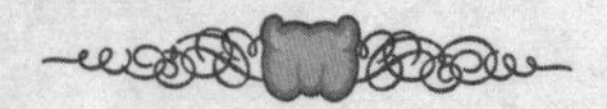

On the bridge of the *Rhapsody 2* the Supers and Dr. C. Fingz took their positions as Captain Squirk readied the transportation device to beam them to Jollywood.

'Remember, Super Moshis, we need to find Splutnik

as soon as possible,' Squirk said. 'The *Rhapsody 2*'s readouts indicate the ice melt on Mt. Sillimanjaro is reaching its final, critical stage. It's absolutely vital we continue our mission to investigate the mystery star that is causing it.'

'You can count on the Super Moshis . . . and Dr. C. Fingz,' Poppet assured him.

The Super Moshis and Dr. C. Fingz rematerialized right in the heart of Jollywood's busiest market place. Palm trees swayed in the breeze and exotic aromas filled the air. Everywhere they looked there were stalls heaving with goods and shopkeepers yelling at their top of their lungs.

'I can smell food!' Furi cried, smacking his lips hungrily.

'Wow, there's a lot going on here!' Diavlo exclaimed

as he looked around. 'How will we know where to start looking for Splutnik?'

'I think Dr. C. Fingz is already on to it,' said Katsuma. The rest of the Supers turned to see the antenna on the Zoshling's head buzzing with activity.

'Over this way,' said Fingz, weaving his way hurriedly through the crowds in the market place.

'Don't let him out of your sight!' Katsuma ordered as the Supers chased after the Zoshling.

When they finally caught up with Fingz again he was busy studying a poster of a dancing figure with a huge blue quiff, a moustache and a snazzy white suit pasted on a wall.

'I get a strong Splutnik reading here . . .' Fingz said thoughtfully.

'That's the famous Roxstar, Bobbi SingSong!' cried Poppet. But before the Supers could stop him, Fingz ripped Bobbi's poster right off the wall!

'Dude! OK, so you don't like Bobbi's music,' said Zommer. 'But ripping up his poster . . . ?'

'No, Zom, look! He's uncovered a gate that was hidden under the poster!' Diavlo cried. 'But what's that painted on it? A Snuggly Tiger Cub?

'Yeah – a Blue Jeepers,' said Poppet. 'The Jollywood variety! Best friends with Bobbi SingSong, no less.'

Just then, they heard a cough and turned to find a Blue Jeepers looking up at them.

'Ahem! I see you've found the gate to Bobbi SingSong's Yoga Retreat! This is where the legendary gooperstar goes to relax between tours. Good luck getting in there though – Bobbi only lets in monsters who have jolly good taste in music!'

With that, the Moshling scurried off, disappearing into the crowds.

The Super Moshis frowned. What was that cryptic message supposed to mean?

'Hang on!' cried Poppet. 'What's that?' A weird-looking electrical device had appeared right in front of the gates.

'It's an ancient music-making machine,' explained Fingz. 'It's called a 'record player'. But the speaker part is missing. The horn. We need to find one so it can play music again. I sense that this is the key that will open the gate.'

'Just like the Moshling said! "Jolly good taste in music." OK, gather round, Supers, we need a plan of attack,' Katsuma said. 'Zom, Furi and Poppet, you guys see if you can find a music stall with a horn. Diavlo and Luvli, you two fly over this wall and see if you can spot Splutnik. Fingz and I will stay here and keep an eye on things.'

The Super Moshis split into their groups and disappeared, leaving Katsuma and Fingz to study the gate more closely.

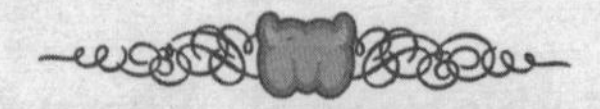

Half an hour later, the Super Moshis gathered once again outside the gate to the Yoga Retreat and everyone had good news to share!

It had taken a bit of running around but Poppet, Furi and Zommer had eventually found the antique horn for the record player. They'd also bought plenty of spicy Jollywood food to take back to the crew of the *Rhapsody 2*. That's if Furi didn't gobble it up first!

Luvli and Diavlo had completed their fly-over of the Yoga Retreat and had glimpsed someone they thought must be Splutnik.

'Excellent work, everyone,' said Katsuma proudly. 'Let's attach this horn and fire up the record player. We've got to get inside this Yoga Retreat and score ourselves some Enlightenment!'

'Hang on, is that Jollywood food I can smell?' Furi asked excitedly.

'Mmmmm, that chow smells awesome!' Zommer agreed.

'Are you two trying to wind me up?' Poppet asked huffily.

'The only one here winding something up is Katsuma!' Luvli laughed. The Supers watched with interest as Katsuma cranked the handle on the side of the record player.

At the first turn of the handle the music poured slowly from the horn, like hot toffee. At the second turn of the handle, it blasted out much too quickly.

The gates to the Yoga Retreat didn't budge.

'You need to get the speed right so Bobbi knows you're musical!' Diavlo hollered. 'That sounds like Iggy Chomp on helium!'

Katsuma slowed his cranking until the music sounded just right.

'Look, the gate is opening!' Poppet cried. 'You did it, Katsuma. We're in!'

The Super Moshis and Dr. C. Fingz hurried though the gates of the Yoga Retreat.

Chapter 6

RESCUING SPLUTNIK

Inside, a stone courtyard was surrounded by high walls, lush plants and beautiful flowers. Soothing pipe music and soft bird calls filled the air and the smell of incense hung heavy on the breeze. The Supers had to admit, it was very relaxing – but they had no time for meditation.

Thanks to Luvli and Diavlo's earlier surveillance mission, Splutnik was exactly where the Super Moshis expected to find him, right in the middle of the retreat. What they weren't expecting however was to see him hovering in mid-air in a trance-like state, accompanied

by Bobbi SingSong and a huge blue creature with massive feet and hands, an enormous belly and an absolutely tiny head!

'Hello!' said the gooperstar, stepping forward politely as the Super Moshis and Fingz entered the courtyard. 'I'm Bobbi SingSong and this is my guru, Big Chief Tiny Head. Welcome to my rrrretreat. How can I help you?'

But Big Chief Tiny Head looked less pleased to see them. 'Who you? How you get in here?' he shouted, his feather headdress bristling.

'Splutnik!' Fingz blurted involuntarily as he caught sight of his friend. 'What have you done to him?'

The Big Chief frowned.

'He in trance, what it look like?' he growled. 'Now answer question – who you? What you doing here?'

'We're the Super Moshis and that's Dr. C. Fingz,' explained Poppet, pointing to the worried Zoshling. 'We've come to rescu . . . er . . . to find our friend Splutnik and take him back to his ship, the *Rhapsody 2*.'

'I am confused,' said Bobbi, turning to the Big Chief. 'I thought you said this meditating wwwwwonder was a friend of yours, Big Chief?'

The guru shuffled his feet uncomfortably and looked at his naked wrist. 'Oh, look at time! I have biggum hula lesson in five minutes! Must no be late – bye!'

And with that the big blue Big Chief Tiny Head raced quickly out of the courtyard, his Hawaiian shirt flapping behind him in the breeze.

'My guru doesn't dilly-dally,' explained Bobbi as he nodded at the retreating figure. 'But don't let his manner fool you. His wisdom has helped me through many tough times. Everyone should have a guru.'

'What happened to his head?' Zommer asked

curiously. 'His body looks normal, but his head . . . it's totally tiny!'

'He got into an argument with a Woolly Blue Hoodoo and to punish him the Hoodoo shrank his head to the size of a pea,' replied Bobbi matter-of-factly.

'Yeah, that sounds about right,' Furi said, remembering their earlier encounter with the excitable Hoodoo tribes in the Unknown Zone.

'As our bro Pocito the Mini Mangler would say, "those Hoodoo are craaaaaaazy-locoooooo!"' said Zommer, tapping his head. Furi giggled.

'Ahem!' Katsuma cleared his throat. 'Anyway . . . Bobbi, how do we bring Splutnik out of this trance?'

'You want to bring him out of it?' Bobbi asked in astonishment. 'But it's the aim of everyone here to reach an advanced state of Brrrr-vana! Your friend was lucky enough to get some private lessons from Big Chief Tiny Head and totally transcended – he's been in this trance ever since. But that was a long time ago now . . .'

Fingz looked worriedly at his friend floating high in the air.

'We need to get him down. Is there a way to do that?' he asked.

'I know there is a mantra you can use,' Bobbi said.

'What's a "mantra"?' asked Luvli.

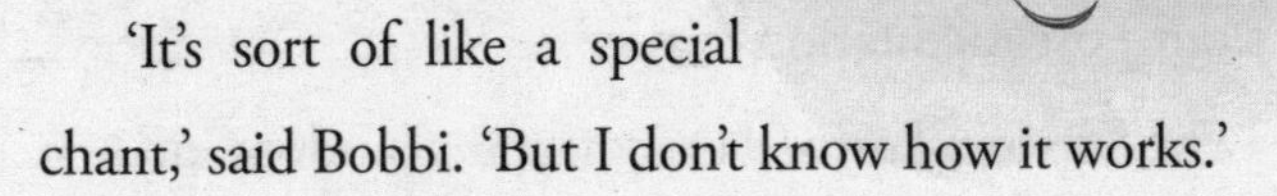

'It's sort of like a special chant,' said Bobbi. 'But I don't know how it works.'

'Let us give it a try,' Diavlo said. 'How does the mantra go?'

Bobbi looked reluctant to tell them, but the concerned look on Fingz's face seemed to make up his mind.

'*A smell quite right, an ear's delight, a touch so light,*' he recited slowly. 'As I say, I don't know how it works . . .'

A silence descended on the group as they mulled over the words of Bobbi's mantra.

'OK, let's look at this logically,' Katsuma said. 'The first bit is about smelling and the last bit is

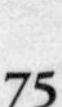

about touching. So the second part is probably about hearing, right?'

'I think so too,' agreed Poppet.

'Me too! But the only thing I can hear is my tummy rumbling!' Furi groaned, rubbing his belly and licking his lips. 'It's that cauldron of bubbling yumminess over there – it's making my mouth water. It smells soooo delicious!'

'That's a local Jollywood specialty,' explained Bobbi. 'It's our post-meditation snack.'

The Supers all turned to look at the outdoor kitchen

set up in one corner of the courtyard. Mouth-watering smells were coming from a large pot of food simmering over an open fire.

'You're a genius, Furi, that's the answer to the first clue – "a smell quite right"!' Luvli yelped. 'Take the lid off that pot, Zom. Grab that portable fan over there, Diavlo. We need to blow those scrumptious cooking smells up to Splutnik!'

The Supers did as Luvli asked then stood back to watch eagerly as the delicious steam from the pot wafted up to the spaced-out Zoshling.

'It's working! Splutnik just sank a couple of feet!' Dr. C. Fingz cried happily.

'OK! The next thing is 'an ear's delight', which we think is about hearing,' said Poppet. 'So that seems to point to music. Does anyone see an instrument anywhere around here?'

The Super Moshis began hunting around the courtyard.

'What about this?' Zommer called excitedly, grabbing

a spatula from a shelf near the fire. He began hitting the cooking pot as hard as he could.

'That is not a delight!' Poppet giggled.

'I can see another thing in that jar, Zom, what is it?' Diavlo called from across the courtyard.

Zommer reached up and took down the other item from the shelf.

'Ooh, ooh! It's a flute! Nice spot, Diavlo!' he said, waving the instrument in the air.

'Lemme have a go!' Furi shouted, bustling over to Zommer. 'I should be good at this, I'm an expert at blowing my own horn!'

'And you're full of hot air!' Zommer snickered, handing Furi the flute to play.

Tootle-lootle-toot! Tooot-lootle-totooly!

Everyone watched expectantly to see how Splutnik would react.

'He's dropped another couple of feet, Super Moshis!' Dr. C. Fingz shouted gleefully. 'I can just about reach him!'

Furi brought his little tune to a close and winked.

'For I'm a jolly good fellow, I deserve lots of barfmallow!' he sang tunelessly.

'Er . . . yeah you are, Furi,' Katsuma grinned. 'And you'll get a reward later. But right now we have to work out the last line of the mantra "A touch so light".'

'What has a light touch?' Poppet muttered, looking around the courtyard.

'A ghost!' Zommer blurted.

'A cloud!' Furi suggested.

'As light as a . . . ' Bobbi fiddled with his neat little moustache as he thought it over. 'As light as a . . . balloon? No. As light as Mice Krispies? No! As light as a . . . feather. A FEATHER! I have it, Super Moshis, a feather!'

'Bobbi's right! Split up and look for a feather!' Katsuma cried.

The Super Moshis began to hunt around.

'FOUND IT!' Luvli called from the treetops. 'There's a nest in this tree with a load of feathers inside!'

She carefully chose the longest one she could find

and flew down to the hovering Splutnik.

'Here goes . . .' she said and with the very tip of the

feather Luvli tickled the Zoshling's feet.

First Splutnik squirmed and then he giggled and then he floated slowly down to land gently on the cobblestoned courtyard.

'W-w-where am I?' he asked in a dazed voice, slowly opening his eyes and looking around in confusion.

'This is Bobbi SingSong's Yoga Retreat,' grinned Fingz. 'This is Bobbi and these are the Super Moshis. We've come to take you home to the *Rhapsody 2*.'

'The *Rhapsody 2*? A Yoga Retreat?' Splutnik repeated vaguely.

'Yes. Don't worry, we'll be home soon,' Fingz said soothingly as he laid his hand on Splutnik's forehead. 'You'll be OK in a moment. We just need to get your things and . . . hang on, where's your jetpack?'

'Jetpack?' Splutnik repeated in a faint voice. But suddenly his bright orange eyes began to focus.

'My jetpack! Now I remember!' he cried.

'What do you mean, Splutnik?' Fingz asked.

'The big blue thing! The fat one! The Hawaiian

shirt guy!' Splutnik blurted.

Zommer and Furi snickered.

'You mean my guru, Big Chief Tiny Head?' Bobbi frowned at the giggling Supers.

Splutnik turned to Bobbi and began to nod furiously.

'Yes! He put me in a trance so he could steal my jetpack!' he squeaked. 'It's all coming back to me now!'

Chapter 7

BOBBI SINGSONG'S DANCE-OFF

'You must be mistaken,' said Bobbi in disbelief. 'My guru would never do a thing like that.'

'He did!' Splutnik insisted. 'I need that jetpack back! We can't let our sophisticated Zoshling technology fall into the wrong hands.'

Splutnik's huge eyes flashed menacingly and his little purple brain, visible through his transparent head, throbbed in anger.

'OK, don't worry, we're going to get it back,' said Poppet kindly. 'Where would we find this Big Chief Tiny Head?'

'He's always at the mountaintop temple,' said Splutnik, jumping up and down impatiently and pointing to a mysterious looking building high above the yoga retreat.

'We're on our way,' said Poppet.

'I don't believe my guru would do anything to harm anyone,' Bobbi kept insisting, as the Supers and the Zoshlings climbed the many steps that led to the temple. 'You don't know him like I do. He is full of wisdom.'

'I'd like to be full of something,' Furi grumbled. 'I'm starving! Do you think I could have one of those Silly Chillis we bought at the Jollywood market, Poppet?'

'No, Furi,' Poppet replied shortly. 'You know we bought those to take back to the *Rhapsody 2*.'

Furi snorted in annoyance.

'If they hadn't scoffed all the ship's supplies they wouldn't need these snacks,' he huffed.

'We haven't scoffed anything,' snapped Dr. C. Fingz. 'The food has been disappearing and no one knows where to. It's like there's a stowaway onboard stealing all our food!'

'A likely story,' Furi mumbled under his breath.

Fingz frowned.

'Both Sprockett and Hubbs insist they've heard someone sneaking around the ship during the night when we Zoshlings have all been tucked up in bed,' he said.

'Shhh,' Katsuma shushed suddenly. 'We've reached the temple. It would be better if we could catch Big Chief Tiny Head by surprise.'

'BWUHAHAHAAHAHAHAHA!' a deep voice boomed from inside the temple. 'Only surprise you going to get is when you find out the extent of my plan, super simpletons!'

With the element of surprise lost, the Supers, Zoshlings and Bobbi entered the temple to find Big Chief Tiny Head waiting for them.

'Ahaha! I see you release your little friend from trance,' he chuckled, nodding at Splutnik.

'Oh! So you admit you put him in a trance?' Bobbi said angrily.

'Of course!' Big Chief shrugged, sipping on a cup of Bungle Jungle Juice.

'I want some answers!' Bobbi spluttered. 'You tricked me into thinking you were a guru!'

Big Chief Tiny Head shook his tiny head disappointedly.

'You easy to fool, stupid Bobbi. I just needed time to study Zoshling technology.' He gestured to Splutnik's missing jetpack in the corner of the temple. 'Pretending to be guru gave me good opportunity.'

'Why did you want to study Splutnik's jetpack?' Poppet asked.

Big Chief Tiny Head shook his head again and began to laugh.

'BWUHAHAHAHAHA!! You no idea who you dealing with, Super Moshis!' he growled menacingly.

The Super Moshis exchanged worried looks. Big Chief Tiny Head might have looked funny – with his loud Hawaiian shirt, tiny head and exotic drink complete with paper umbrella – but he was quite scary really!

'You won't get away with this Tiny Head!' Bobbi shouted furiously. 'I mean to settle this here and now!'

Big Chief Tiny Head's eyes narrowed. 'A dance-off?' he asked.

'What else?!' Bobbi replied angrily.

'If the Super Moshis would be so kind as to provide the music . . .' He pointed to several bongo drums stored at one end of the temple. 'Then we'll begin!'

'Fine!' Big Chief Tiny Head sneered, taking a big swig of Bungle Jungle Juice.

The Super Moshis took their positions behind the bongos, and Bobbi and Big Chief Tiny Head took to the floor, which suddenly lit up with multicoloured lights like a disco.

'Um, perhaps Splutnik and I should take over the musical duties,' Dr. C. Fingz suggested hesitantly. 'After

all, we are from Symphonia, the most musical world in the Swooniverse . . .'

'Ahhh, yes, good point,' Katsuma replied.

Meanwhile, Bobbi and Big Chief Tiny Head circled each other on the dance floor, their eyes never leaving the other's face. This was shaping up to be the most competitive dance-off Jollywood had ever seen!

‘Hit it!’ Bobbi cried suddenly and the Zoshlings began to play.

With every beat of the drums Bobbi kicked out his legs and wiggled his hips. He waved his arms and waggled his head. He busted moves not usually seen this far west of Monstro City.

While Bobbi danced, the Super Moshis cheered and whistled and boogied right along with him. They were all in it together – the Moshis, the Zoshlings and the Moshling!

'Well done, Bobbi!' Luvli cheered as the song came to an end.

'You totally nailed it!' Zommer yelled.

'You can't beat that, Big Chief Tiny Brain!' Diavlo jeered.

Big Chief Tiny Head frowned and sipped his drink thoughtfully. Bobbi SingSong had better moves and the chief knew it.

'You tore up dance floor, Bobbi,' he said with grudging admiration, putting his drink aside. 'But it not matter. I got what I came for. **BUH-WAHAHAHAHAA!**'

And instead of assuming his dance position, Big Chief Tiny Head fiddled with a small device strapped to his wrist and promptly disappeared.

'Cosmic crumbs! Did you see that?' Splutnik exclaimed in amazement.

'I'm afraid we're all too familiar with that disappearing act!' Poppet replied. 'First it was Frau Now BrownKau at the Sandy Drain Hotel.'

'And then Candy the Clown aka Sweet Tooth at the Cirque du BonBon!' Furi chimed in.

'I'm sensing a pattern here,' said Katsuma. 'What did Big Chief Tiny Head mean when he said we didn't know who we were dealing –'

A loud grinding noise, like stone rubbing against stone, drowned out the rest of Katsuma's sentence.

'What is making that noise?' Luvli shouted worriedly over the din. 'It sounds like it's coming from the ceiling!'

Everyone looked up in astonishment.

'That's weird! Did the temple ceiling always have spikes sticking out of it?' Zommer yelled.

'Hmmm, I don't think so, Zom!' Diavlo cried, struggling to make himself heard over the racket. 'I'm not sure it was moving towards us like that before either!'

They watched in horror as the spiky ceiling began lowering to the floor.

'We have to get out of here or we'll be flattened like Jollywood chapattis!' Bobbi howled.

'Not if we're skewered like chicken kebabs on those spikes first!' Katsuma exclaimed.

'We're done for!' Furi moaned. 'And I never did collect a full set of Techie Moshlings!'

'Brace yourselves everyone!' Poppet commanded. 'Keep clear of the spikes and we'll try pushing against the ceiling!'

The brave adventurers put their arms above their heads and screwed their eyes up tight against their impending doom. In their hearts they feared there was no way to stop the ceiling turning them from Super Moshis into super goo . . .

Chapter 8

READY FOR LAUNCH

Furi, the tallest of the Supers, was the first to feel the cold stone of the ceiling bump against his fingertips.

'Be brave, Super Moshis!' he hollered. 'It's almost – hey, whaaaaat?'

A bolt of orange light suddenly flashed from a corner of the room and hit the ceiling, filling the room with a bright glow and bringing the death trap to a halt.

Katsuma's eyes snapped open.

'W-w-we're saved, Supers!' he shrieked in delight. 'The ceiling has – ELDER FURI!'

'The ceiling has Elder Furi?' Diavlo opened his eyes and looked around in confusion. 'What do you mean, Katsu – ELDER FURI!'

Now everyone opened their eyes to find Elder Furi standing in the corner of the temple, his staff still glowing bright orange.

'You're a long way from home, my Super Moshis,' he said as the monsters crowded around him and all began talking at once.

'Calm yourselves, my Supers, and I will explain,' Elder Furi said gently. 'But first, who are our new friends?'

Splutnik, Fingz and Bobbi approached the great Moshi leader.

'Splutnik and Dr. C. Fingz are part of a Zoshling space mission that was sent to investigate a mysterious star threatening our world!' Poppet explained.

'But their ship, the *Rhapsody 2*, was biffed out of the sky by a giant glove and the crew went missing when it crashed on Music Island,' Diavlo added.

'We've been helping them ever since,' Luvli added.

'And this is Bobbi SingSong, Jollywood's most famous gooperstar!' Furi grinned as Bobbi and Elder Furi shook hands.

'And what about you, Elder Furi, where have you been?' Katsuma asked.

'After our last big battle against Dr. Strangeglove I was sucked up into C.L.O.N.C.'s plane, *Scare Force One*,' Elder Furi began. 'Luckily I was able to escape through a window and use my cape to parachute to safety. Unfortunately I landed in a virtually uninhabited part of Music Island and I've been wandering around trying to find my way back to Monstro City ever since. We've all found each other again now though.' He smiled serenely.

'And we have too!' Fingz grinned, putting his hand on Splutnik's shoulder. 'I'll contact Captain Squirk via my antenna and arrange to get us beamed back to the *Rhapsody 2*!'

'What about you, Bobbi, will you come back with us?' Luvli asked sweetly.

Bobbi SingSong looked at the Zoshlings and nodded enthusiastically.

'Yes please! I can't let truly talented bongo players

like Splutnik and Dr. C. Fingz get away. I need them to perform on my next album.' He grinned delightedly.

As our adventurers rematerialized on the bridge of the *Rhapsody 2*, Captain Squirk rushed forward to greet them.

'Splutnik! My dear, Splutnik!' the Zoshling whooped, tears of happiness filling his little round eyes.

First Officer Ooze hurried over to join the captain, Dr. C. Fingz and Splutnik and the little creatures hugged each other and beamed joyfully.

'Wonderful! A four-piece band!' Bobbi SingSong said gleefully, surveying the entire Zoshling crew.

'Hey!' said Poppet suddenly. 'I almost forgot the food!'

'Food?' cried Captain Squirk, jumping up and down excitedly.

Poppet emptied her backpack of all the yummy treats she'd bought at Jollywood market and everyone fell silent for a few minutes as they tucked in.

'Burp! That Pepper Popcorn really hit the spot,' Captain Squirk sighed contentedly, brushing the crumbs from his space tunic.

Tingaling gave a little meow of distaste and everybody laughed.

Squirk blushed.

'Pardon me. I think it's time to get back on track.'

'The *Rhapsody 2* is ready to launch, Sir,' First Officer Ooze said, standing up. 'We must resume our mission to explore the origins of the mystery star and see what we can do to guarantee the safety of the Moshi world.'

'Good, quite right' said Squirk with a nod. 'If you'd be interested in seeing our launch sequence, Super Moshis, you're most welcome to come down to the engine room and observe.'

'That's very kind of you, Captain, but I must get back to Monstro City immediately. I've been away too long already!' Elder Furi replied. 'But I'm sure my Super Moshis would love to see it.'

The Supers all nodded happily.

Captain Squirk smiled.

'Then we will see you in the engine room when you're ready, Super Moshis,' he said. 'Come, Zoshlings, we must take our positions. Sprockett and Hubbs, you stay on the bridge and await further orders.'

The Zoshlings departed for the engine room while the Super Moshis and Bobbi SingSong exited the spaceship.

'Come back to Monstro City as soon as you can, Supers,' said Elder Furi gravely. 'We have much to discuss regarding your adventures!'

'Like what, Elder Furi?' Zommer asked.

'Oh, like why Frau Now BrownKau was bottling Ooze's cosmic gloop at the Sandy Drain Hotel?' replied Elder Furi.

'What was Sweet Tooth doing working at a circus and why was it using Dr. C. Fingz to find out how many Moshlings circus patrons had collected?' Katsuma added.

'And don't forget Big Chief Tiny Head said "you've no idea who you're dealing with",' Poppet chimed in. 'I don't think he was talking about himself. I get the feeling there's something sinister behind all of it . . .'

'Yeah! And BrownKau, Sweet Tooth and the Chief all disappeared the same way. By activating a wrist teleportation device!' Furi said.

'Ye-es, there's an unmistakeable smell of C.L.O.N.C.

in the air . . .' Elder Furi said thoughtfully. 'We shall get to the bottom of all this mystery, Super Moshis, you can be sure of it!'

Once Elder Furi had departed and Bobbi had wandered off with Tingaling to stretch their legs, the Super Moshis made their way back onboard and down to the engine room.

'WOW!' Katsuma's jaw hung open in amazement as he walked through the door.

'I didn't expect that!' Luvli cried in astonishment.

'They're . . . they're . . . the Zoshlings are part of the ship!' Poppet gasped.

The four Zoshling crewmembers stood on top of platforms that were plugged directly into the ship's engine.

'Correct, Super Moshis!' Captain Squirk grinned. 'We are part of the ship, just as the ship is part of us. To initiate the launch sequence we need to fire the engines with some cosmic tunes!'

Barely had the words left his lips when cosmic music

filled the engine room. The Zoshlings rose and fell on their platforms depending on the pitch of the music.

'Interstellar incredibleness!' Furi exclaimed.

Soon the music sequences were complete and the engines ready to blast the *Rhapsody 2* back into space.

Captain Squirk jumped down off his platform and pushed a button to patch through to the bridge.

Sprockett and Hubbs filled the big screen on the wall opposite.

'Sprockett, Hubbs? Launch sequence is complete and we're ready for blast off,' Captain Squirk said. 'But please wait until the Super Moshis have left the ship to press the launch button.'

On the bridge, Sprockett turned to Hubbs and scratched his bubble-head.

'Er . . . did he just say "press the launch button"?' he asked.

'Did he? Oh, OK.' Hubbs shrugged and pressed the large button marked 'launch'.

'Noooooooooo! I didn't –' Captain Squirk shouted. But it was too late!

Chapter 9

EVIL REVEALED

The *Rhapsody 2* shuddered as the gangplank retracted and its landing gear folded back up into the ship.

The big screen in the engine room suddenly filled with static and went black.

The Super Moshis looked at each other.

'Uh-oh . . .' Diavlo said, his red face turning quite pale.

Slowly the spaceship rose into the air, hovered for a moment and sped off at hyper-speed up, up, up into the Way-Outta-Sphere!

Back on the ground, Bobbi SingSong and Tingaling watched until the *Rhapsody 2* was nothing but a tiny speck in the sky.

'I'll say this for the Zoshlings,' Bobbi said as he reached over to gently ruffle Tingaling's head. 'They certainly don't dilly-dally.'

'Meow!' she replied, pawing at his moustache.

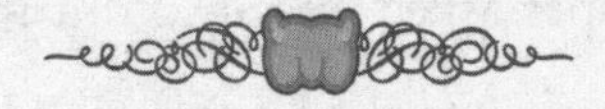

Captain Squirk rolled his eyes and let out a long-suffering sigh.

'Everyone wait here,' he said. 'I'll go up to the bridge and turn the *Rhapsody 2* around.'

The Super Moshis and the rest of the Zoshlings waited until Squirk had left the engine room before they began giggling uncontrollably.

'It is quite f-f-f-unny,' Furi snickered. 'The look on H-h-h-ubbs's face when he saw what he'd done.'

Suddenly the big screen spluttered into life again and what the Super Moshis saw made their blood run cold.

'This is your Captain speaking . . .' a sinister voice cackled.

'Dr. Strangeglove!' The Super Moshis all cried at once.

'Mwah-ha-haaaaaaaaaaaa! Hello, Super Meddlers!' Strangeglove said. 'Thanks for finding me this spaceship and gathering the crew! I couldn't have done it without you!'

'Huh?' Poppet asked angrily. 'You mean to tell us that you followed us to the *Rhapsody 2*? Have you been aboard the whole time?'

'Ohhhh, I feel offended that nobody noticed little old me,' Strangeglove replied, pulling an exaggerated sad face. 'Who do you think was eating all the ship's food supplies, you heroic half-wits? Who do you think left that oh-so-obvious note stuck to the ship's windscreen telling you that the key to the ship was at the Hoodoo Hideaway? And the poster advertising Dr. C. Fingz's act at the Cirque du BonBon? Me again!'

'Whatever your evil plan is, we'll put a stop to it, Strangeglove!' Diavlo growled.

Dr. Strangeglove rolled his eyes dismissively.

'Whatever, Super Piano, or whatever it is you call yourself,' he sighed. 'Anyway, I've taken control of the ship, so enjoy the ride. Buh-bye!'

The screen went blank again.

'RARRRRRR!' Furi hollered in frustration.

'We need to work fast,' Katsuma said, quickly patching through to the bridge. 'Captain Squirk, did you see what we just saw? We need to find out where on the ship Dr. Strangeglove is hiding!'

The screen crackled and popped and Squirk's concerned face appeared.

'I saw, Super Moshis! The ship's sensors show Dr. Strangeglove has locked himself into First Officer Ooze's greenhouse. Study the ship's plan and you'll see where I mean,' he said worriedly.

A large plan of the *Rhapsody 2* came up on screen.

'Don't worry, Captain, we'll catch him!' Poppet said determinedly. She raced to the door of the engine room and made a shocking discovery. 'It's locked.

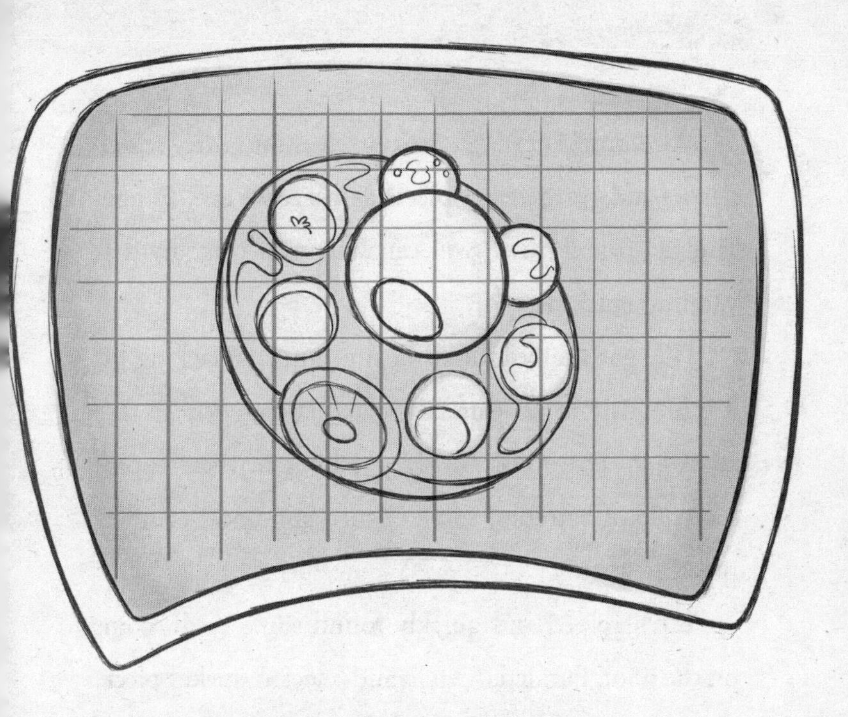

Dr. Strangeglove has shut us in!'

One by one the Super Moshis tried the door. But it was no use: the locking motor was jammed.

'We're wasting time!' Luvli cried in alarm.

'Wait, I've just remembered! We hid three key pieces somewhere in the engine room for emergencies such as this!' Splutnik exclaimed. 'When you put them together in that hold in the door, they look like my face. We just need to find them . . .'

'Awesome! Let's organize ourselves into three search parties and get these key pieces as fast as we can,' Poppet said. 'Furi and Luvli, you can start over there by that vending machine.'

'We got the best task!' Furi grinned, smacking his lips hungrily as he neared the glass cabinet. But his face soon fell. There was hardly anything in there except a couple of batteries, some bottled sun and . . . a key piece!

Luvli yelped and quickly found some credit coins on the floor. Furi fed them in and selected the key piece, plus some spare batteries and the bottled sun for good measure. 'We've got one!' he called excitedly, running over to join the others. 'And I got this stuff too!'

'Batteries! We need those to power this giant magnet to pull down that big key piece up there,' said Poppet, pointing to a huge circle above the door.

'And we need the bottled sun to power this engine – the third piece is stuck inside it!' cried Katsuma.

ABC
123

The adventurers powered up the magnet and engine, and the two pieces were soon in their hands. They arranged them hurriedly in the circular space, sliding them into place until they resembled Splutnik's face – and the door slid open!

'The Super Moshis and the Zoshlings make a great team!' First Office Ooze smiled as he raced through towards the greenhouse.

'Yeah!' Zommer agreed, fist bumping the little Zoshling. 'We totally nailed that key situation. Now it's time to bring Strangeglove's little game to an end.'

'Mwahahahaha! Not so fast, Super Freak!' Dr. Strangeglove's face appeared again on the communication screen above the door and his voice boomed out over the speakers. 'All is going according to my evil plan.'

'You can't fool us, Strangeglove,' Katsuma scowled. 'You were marooned on Music Island, so something obviously went wrong with your "evil plan".' Katsuma sketched air quotes around the last two words.

'Bah! I didn't foresee C.L.O.N.C. throwing me off

Scare Force One, it's true, but that was only a minor blip. Luckily you super snoops came along and led me straight to this ship! Mwa-hahahahaha! Anyway, must dash. Enjoy the trip!'

Fuzz filled the communication screen and when it cleared Captain Squirk's face had replaced Dr. Strangeglove's.

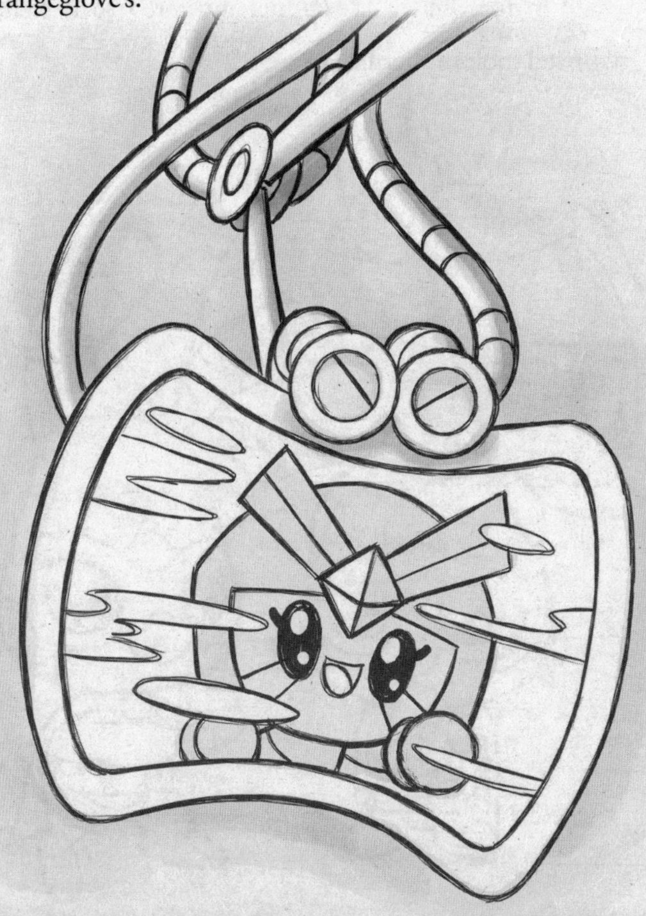

'You're outside the greenhouse, Super Moshis, and the good news is that I've managed to unlock the door! Dr. Strangeglove neglected to disable the central override lock that opens all the doors on the ship. He thinks he knows the *Rhapsody 2*, but nobody knows this ship like I do!' Squirk said proudly.

'Or does he . . . ?' Poppet muttered to herself, a worried look on her face.

'What is it, Poppet?' Katsuma asked.

'It's just . . . I can't imagine Strangeglove wouldn't be all over that central locking system,' Poppet replied. 'Maybe I'm imagining things, but . . .'

She trailed off and with a shrug turned her attention back to the communication screen.

'There's one problem though,' Squirk was saying. 'Strangeglove is no longer in the greenhouse. According to the ship's sensors he's holed up in my quarters. Use the greenhouse's back exit to follow him; it's the quickest way! I'll go around the other way – he won't find it so easy to slip through our fingers this time!'

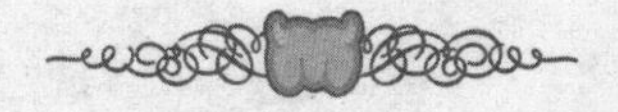

The Super Moshis gaped in astonishment at the thick, tangled greenery that covered the walls of the greenhouse.

'Dude! It's like the Gombala Gombala Jungle in here!' Zommer exclaimed.

'Ye-es, I've been so busy helping with repairs to the *Rhapsody 2* that I'd no idea my plants had grown so wild,' First Officer Ooze explained, blushing. 'We'll need to mix up some cosmic weed removal potion to find the back exit! For this we'll need to gather six Mexican Jumping Beans, one Electric Boogaloo

Mushroom, some freshly picked Sausage and Mash and a few sun-dried Blue Grape Raisins.'

'Mmmmm, Sausage and Mash!' Furi beamed happily.

Chapter 10

THE LAST LAUGH

With time of the essence, the adventurers split up into groups, each one responsible for finding a particular ingredient.

Katsuma and Furi were in charge of planting and harvesting the sausage seed for the Sausage and Mash tree. Luckily they didn't need very much of this ingredient because Furi greedily gobbled it up almost as fast as it grew!

Under Ooze's watchful eye, Poppet and Zommer took control of electrifying the Boogaloo Mushroom in the greenhouse's Weather Machine. Let's just say

Zommer's hair was standing just a little bit straighter after the machine's various lightning strikes.

Diavlo and Splutnik had fun rounding up the lively Mexican Jumping Beans, dancing alongside them to the exotic sounds of the Mariachi Plants.

Luvli and Dr. C. Fingz picked the Blue Grapes easily enough but the recipe for the potion required them to be sun-dried. Once again Ooze and his Weather Machine came to the rescue. With controls set to 'sun' the Blue Grapes dried up before their very eyes.

Finally the potion was ready. All that they needed to do now was pour it into the Weed Buster 200X and get bustin' those weeds! Squirt! Squirt! Squirt!

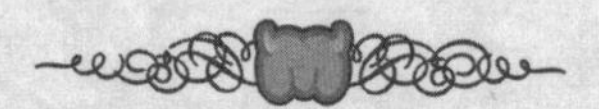

Soon the back wall of the greenhouse was weed-free and the back exit uncovered.

'Excellent work, everyone,' Katsuma said, striding over to the door. 'Now let's get after Strangeglo –'

He stopped mid-sentence and gave the door a pull.

'Gah! It's locked!' Katsuma snorted in disgust. 'We did all that weed removal business for nothing!'

'What about getting out through this vent here beside the door?' Splutnik suggested, pointing to a small square vent cut into the wall.

The Super Moshis turned to look at him doubtfully.

'I don't think we'll fit through there actually, Splutnik . . .' Poppet replied uncertainly.

'Oh, I think we will,' Splutnik replied with a wink. 'Ooze?'

Ooze stepped forward and flung some of his cosmic goo onto the vent.

'Intergalactic ingeniousness! The vent's growing!' Diavlo exclaimed.

Soon it was big enough for everyone to comfortably fit through.

'Wow! I love our Moshi world, but Symphonia? With your crazy cosmic goo and banging Weather Machine, you Zoshings really have it sorted!' Furi grinned.

'Super Moshis, I got here too late!' Captain Squirk cried as the adventurers raced through the back door of his quarters. 'Strangeglove got out of the room and locked me in! So don't let that door behind you . . .'

The door through which the Supers and Zoshlings had just entered clanged shut behind them.

' . . . close.'

'Now we're all locked in!' Katsuma growled in frustration.

A communication screen suddenly lowered from the ceiling and burst into life. Dr. Strangeglove looked smugly down at them, his moustache curling with evil delight.

'Mwa-hah-haaaaa! See what I did there? Locked you up tight!' he crowed triumphantly. 'Give up, you bumbling buffoons. You'll never catch me. I'm an evil genius, remember?'

'Don't be too sure of yourself – 'Poppet began to say before Strangeglove rudely cut her off.

'Talk to the glove!' he snapped, cutting communications.

Captain Squirk meanwhile was busy tapping into the ship's plan.

'The motion sensors indicate Strangeglove is in . . .

the escape pod!' He yelped. 'He's trying to get off the *Rhapsody 2*!'

'Is there any way out of here, Captain Squirk?' Diavlo asked hopefully. 'Hidden keys? Door opening potions?'

'We'll need to reset the terminals,' Squirk replied quickly. 'I'll get busy over here. The rest of you take care of the Arcade Machine, the Pink Terminal and Jokebot the Robot.'

'Leave the Arcade Machine to me,' Zommer said. 'Remember how I totally ruled Hoodoo Pong back in the Unknown Zone?'

'You're the game master, Zom!' Furi replied, punching the air excitedly as he, Fingz, Ooze and Splutnik gathered around to watch. 'Get ready to witness some magic, Zoshlings!'

'And I'll take the Pink Terminal because I'm . . . well, I'm pink!' Poppet announced.

'We'll help,' Luvli added as she and Diavlo joined Poppet on the other side of the room.

'I guess that leaves me and you eh, Jokebot?' Katsuma

smiled up at the large robot parked beside Squirk.

Jokebot stared back at him without replying.

'Helloooo in there,' Katsuma called, knocking tinnily on the robot's body. 'Anyone home?'

Captain Squirk glanced up from reprogramming the terminal.

'You'll need to insert Jokebot's humour chip,' he explained, pointing at a metal bow tie lying on a bench beside the robot. 'I take it out whenever I power him down. You'll soon see why.'

Katsuma gave Squirk a quizzical look as he popped the bow tie onto Jokebot. What was Squirk hinting at?

With a whirr of cogs and a hiss of movement, the robot suddenly came to life, his face lighting up with a green glow.

'I have a new audience! I am Jokebot! *Rhapsody 2*'s on-board robot comedian!' he said in his metallic voice. 'My circuits have been reset, so I am unable to remember all my best jokes. Please help me.'

'Okaaaay . . . sure,' Katsuma replied doubtfully.

'How do you make a tissue dance?' the Jokebot began.

'I know this one, I know this one!' cried Furi from the Arcade Machine. 'You put a little boogie in it. Ahahahahahah!'

'Good one, dude,' Zommer said, pausing at the controls briefly to collapse on the floor in hysterics. The other Super Moshis looked unamused.

'Indeed, that tickled my transistors,' said the Jokebot. He told two more unfunny jokes, twice more Furi knew the dreadful punchlines and twice more, Zommer cried with laughter. Finally, the ordeal came to an end.

'Stand-up comedy retrieval complete, opening doors,' Jokebot announced suddenly.

'All right!' Katsuma yelled exultantly.

'We're done here too!' Poppet called from across the room.

'Yeah, me too!' Zommer added.

Captain Squirk spun around from his console.

'Done!' he cried happily and at that moment the door to his quarters opened with a swoooooosh.

'C'mon, Super Moshis! We've got to get to the escape pod before Strangeglove makes a run for it!' Poppet said, racing for the door.

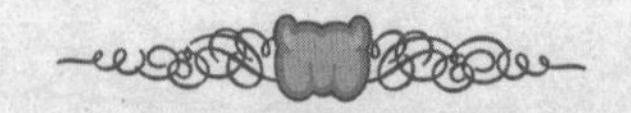

While the Zoshlings rushed to the bridge in order to jam the escape pod's launch sequence, the Super Moshis sprinted to the escape pod itself.

'We're in luck, the door's unlocked,' Diavlo said, spotting the green light over the entrance. 'We have Strangeglove cornered!'

The door slid open and the Super Moshis piled inside to find . . . Scarlet O'Haira the Fluffy Snuggler Moshling!

'Where's Strangeglove?' Furi asked.

As if on cue, the escape pod's communication screen suddenly dropped from the ceiling.

'Mwahahaha! Where indeed?' Strangeglove chuckled. 'I was never in the escape pod, you all-star amateurs! It was that Moshling furball the whole time.'

'Don't think you've outsmarted us, Strangeglove!' Katsuma growled. 'We're not so easy to take for a ride!'

'Oh, but you are, super saps. You're going for a loooooong ride,' Strangeglove replied.

Suddenly the Super Moshis felt the escape pod's engine roar into life.

'Uuuuummmmm, this isn't good,' Luvli frowned as she looked around the tiny one-roomed ship. 'The escape pod has no steering controls. If Strangeglove launches us, we'll be left drifting in space.'

'The not-so-hearty one is right!' Strangeglove snickered delightedly. 'So I suppose all that's left for me to do is say bye bye!'

The Supers exchanged shocked looks. They were utterly helpless!

With a loud clunk the escape pod detached from the *Rhapsody 2* and was flung out into deep space. The Super Moshis crowded around the one tiny window and watched, horrified, as they drifted away from the safety of the spaceship, into the deep darkness of the Swooniverse.

In the silence of space, all the Super Moshis could hear was the sound of Strangeglove's dastardly laugh . . .

MWA-HA-HA-HAAAAAAA!

Continued in the fourth and final book . . .

Don't miss the next exciting Music Island Mission adventure, coming soon in paperback and ebook:

Read an exclusive extract on the next page!

Chapter 1

CRASH LANDING

As the *Rhapsody 2* disappeared completely from view, the Super Moshis and fluffy Moshling Scarlet O'Haira sighed helplessly and slumped to the floor of the escape pod.

'Now that Dr. Strangeglove has gained control of the Zoshlings' ship, who's going to investigate the mysterious star that's threatening our world?' Luvli asked anxiously. 'We're running out of time! Remember what Captain Squirk said? If the ice on Mount Sillimanjaro carries on melting so quickly, it'll only be a matter of days before Monstro City is underwater!'

Katsuma and Poppet frowned. There was nothing they could do to help either the Zoshlings or the Moshi world in their current predicament.

'This escape pod has no steering controls!' Katsuma growled in frustration.

'Er, what do you mean?' asked Poppet nervously, but Katsuma had no time to answer.

'Yeah, and if that wasn't bad enough, we're gonna smash into this huge asteroid,' moaned Furi, pointing at a huge rock ahead of them. 'Talk about having a bad day!'

'W-w-what?!' Poppet raced over to him and gasped as the cratered surface of the asteroid approached at top speed. 'Perplexing planetoids, Furi's right! Guys, things are about to get bumpy! We've got five seconds to execute a team huddle position.'

FIVE!

The Super Moshis and Scarlet flattened themselves to the floor.

FOUR!

They grabbed each others' hands.

THREE!

They closed their eyes tight.

TWO!

They held their breath.

BOOOOOOOM!

Diavlo opened his eyes and looked around at the tangle of wires and bits of broken metal strewn all over the escape pod.

'Is everyone OK?' he asked, dragging himself to his feet and dusting himself down. He could hear spluttery coughs and moans around the escape pod.

'All good here!' Furi groaned.

'Luvli and I are OK, too,' Poppet said, wincing.

Suddenly a horrified cry filled the pod.

'Oh, duuuuude! I've lost an eye!' shrieked Zommer, dropping to his knees to scrabble through the wreckage.

'But you've only ever had one eye, Zom,' Katsuma

said, patting him on the shoulder.

'Oh yeah . . .' Zommer said, standing up slowly and looking at his feet.

'Where's Scarlet O'Haira?' Luvli asked worriedly.

Out of the corner of her eye Poppet saw a bit of plastic from the escape pod's console shuffling across the floor. She lifted it up and smiled. Scarlet was underneath it.

'Yeah, Scarlet is safe, too,' Poppet said.

'Great! Well . . . that could've been a lot worse!' Katsuma said, grinning. 'The only problem appears to be the sound on the communication screen.'

The Supers looked up at it. There was Captain Squirk, looking concerned and mouthing words they couldn't hear.

'We! Can't! Hear! You! Dude!' Furi yelled at the top of his lungs.

Poppet sighed loudly.

'Let's just fix the volume button, shall we?' said Luvli.

'Are you receiving me, Super Moshis?'

Captain Squirk's melodic voice filled the escape pod as Katsuma slotted the final TV fuse back into place. 'Is anybody hurt?'

'We're receiving you, Captain,' Diavlo reassured him.

'Everyone here is OK and the escape pod has only minor damage,' Poppet added. 'So if you could just tell us how to get off this rock . . . ?'

'The *Rhapsody 2*'s computer scans show you've crashed on an asteroid with a highly explosive core,' Captain Squirk began.

The Super Moshis and Scarlet all gasped, before Squirk hurriedly added, 'But don't panic, the surface is quite safe!'

Everyone breathed out loudly.

'What I'm trying to say, badly, is that if you can figure out a way to use this core material to create an explosion beneath the escape pod, you might be able to launch it back into space,' Captain Squirk explained.

'Thanks, Captain. We'll take a look around and

see what we can come up with,' Katsuma said. 'In the meantime, are you and the crew of the *Rhapsody 2* all right? What's Strangeglove up to?'

Squirk frowned.

'We're all OK. Strangeglove has locked us in my quarters,' he replied. 'The weird thing is that he hasn't altered the course I originally set for the ship – we're still heading straight for the mystery star!'

'How odd . . .' mused Poppet.

'Well, we'd better hurry up and get back to you,' said Katsuma. 'Don't worry – the Super Moshis are on the case.'

'Good luck!' said Squirk, and the screen fizzled to black.

The door to the escape pod swoooshed open and the Super Moshis found themselves on the cold, dusty surface of the asteroid.

'If only we'd crash-landed on the moon,' Furi

sighed, rubbing his grumbling tummy as he looked about. 'I hear that's made of cheese. The only thing here is a bunch of stupid rocks!'

'Get your facts right! They're Cosmic Rox!' someone shouted angrily behind him.

The Super Moshis jumped in alarm and spun around to find an elderly green bearded creature frowning at them.

'What are you doing barging your way onto my asteroid?' the figure continued, furiously wagging his finger. 'Insulting my Rox? I'm Wally Warpspeed, the world-famous Cosmic Rox miner, and these rocks aren't stupid, they are highly explosive and so rare, they're worth millions of . . . well . . . Rox, so there!'

'Sorry, Mr. Warpspeed, we crash-landed,' Luvli said, fluttering her eyelashes apologetically. 'And your Cosmic Rox really are wonderful. You must have made a fortune from selling them!'

Wally Warpspeed frowned some more.

'Well, as it happens, no,' he snapped. 'I was all ready to leave with my valuable cargo when I went to take a sip of Fizzy soda and accidentally spilt some. Then, all of a sudden . . . BOOM! The Cosmic Rox exploded and blew my spaceship apart!'

He gestured over his shoulder at the wreckage of his spaceship, drifting slowly away in the distance.

'The only thing it's good for now is keeping Fizzy locked up and out of trouble!' Wally winked cheekily.

'Er . . . riiiight,' Katsuma said doubtfully. 'Well, if you wouldn't mind, we'd like to speak to Fizzy. You see, we need to create an explosion to blast our escape pod back into the Way-Outta-Sphere and Fizzy sounds like just the guy to help us.'

'Well, that would be OK, only I lost the front door handle to my ship ages ago. But if you can find it, you can speak to Fizzy,' Wally shrugged. 'It should be around here somewhere.'

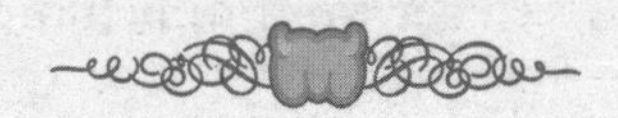

It was clear to the Super Moshis that all those years of mining Cosmic Rox had sent Wally Warpspeed a little nuts.

'He's got Rox up here!' Zommer whispered to Furi, tapping his forehead meaningfully.

'And his ship's in a terrible state!' cried Poppet.

The Moshis gaped at the wreckage. The explosion had sent pieces of metal flying in all directions. Happily though, it didn't take the Supers long to find the door handle amongst the debris. They fixed it back onto the hatch, turned it, and Fizzy burst out with a squeal.

'Phew, thanks!' he cried gratefully. 'I've been stuck in there forever! Wally wants to keep me locked up because I blew up his ship – which I only did once. By accident. It wasn't my fault! It's just when I mix with Cosmic Rox everything goes BOOM!'

Fizzy stopped to draw a breath and Katsuma immediately tried to get word in before he could start talking again!

'So you're Fizzy?' he asked.

Fizzy looked around at the Super Moshis in surprise, as if he hadn't really noticed them before.

'Haha! Sorry. I've been locked in there so long I've lost my manners,' the little drink giggled. 'I'm Fizzy, the Lipsmacking Bubbly. Who are you guys?'

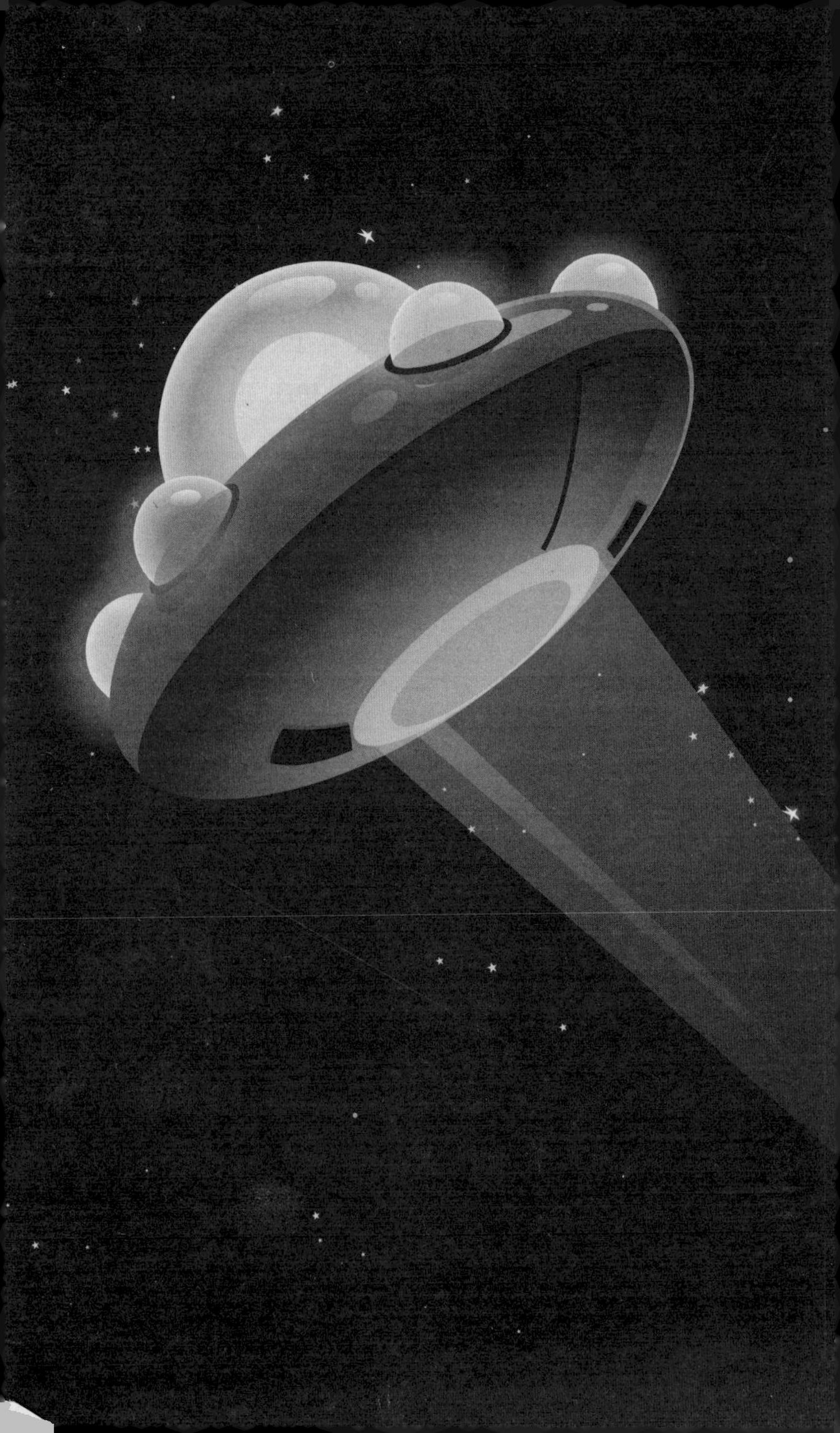